# DINOSAURS DIDN'T HAVE DANCE PARTIES

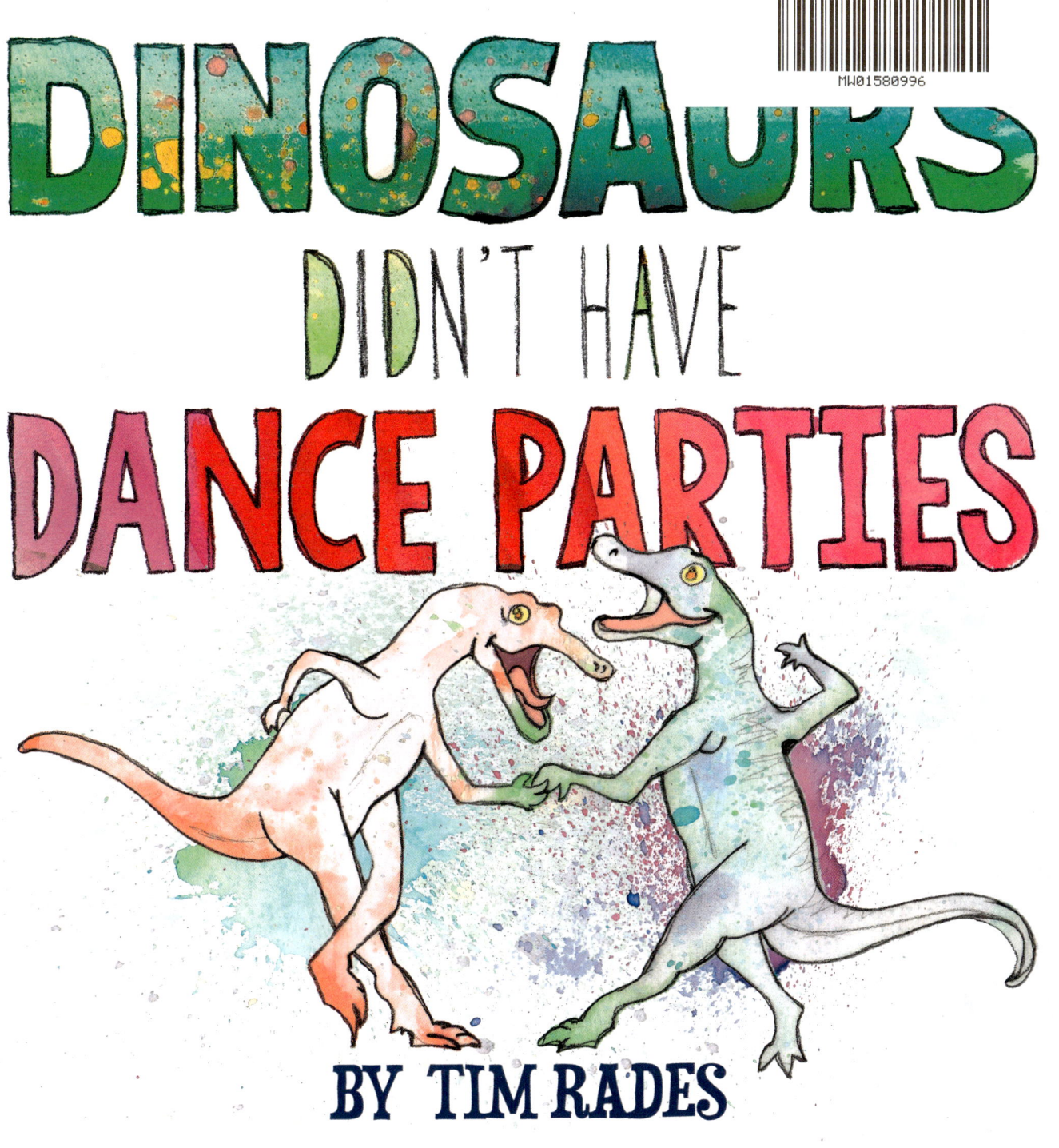

## BY TIM RADES

Copyright © 2020 by Tim Rades

All rights reserved

ISBN-13:978-1-7349552-5-5

To my pal, Thunder Dan

Dinosaurs didn't have dance parties,

'cause there was no music then.

So dinos couldn't do a jig,

or cut a rug with friends.

No Pteranodon Pachanga,

no Diplodocus Disco,

# No Brachiosaurus Breakdance

or Monolophosaurus Mambo.

# No Tangoing Triceratops

or Ceratosaurus Cha Cha.

No Iguanodon doing the robot

or Spinosaurus Samba.

There was no Segnosaurus Salsa,

or Lambeosaurus Line Dancing.

No Chindesaurus Charleston,

and no Brontosaurus Ballet.

So be grateful you have music, to Waltz

or Bunny Hop,

or Frug

or Pasadoble,

Made in the USA
Monee, IL
13 November 2020